COSMO FOR CAPTAIN

Jonathan Emmett

Illustrated by
Peter Rutherford

OXFORD
UNIVERSITY PRESS

OXFORD
UNIVERSITY PRESS

Great Clarendon Street, Oxford, OX2 6DP,
United Kingdom

Oxford University Press is a department of the University of Oxford.
It furthers the University's objective of excellence in research, scholarship,
and education by publishing worldwide. Oxford is a registered trade mark of
Oxford University Press in the UK and in certain other countries

Text © Jonathan Emmett 2002

British Library Cataloguing in Publication Data
Data available

978-0-19-276529-1

1 3 5 7 9 10 8 6 4 2

Paper used in the production of this book is a natural, recyclable product
made from wood grown in sustainable forests. The manufacturing process
conforms to the environmental regulations of the country of origin.

Printed in China

Acknowledgements
Cover and inside illustrations by Peter Rutherford
Background images by Shutterstock
Series editor: Alison Sage

Helping your child to read

Before they start

- Talk about the back cover blurb. What does your child think is going to happen in this story?

- Look at the front cover. What kind of creatures are Cosmo and Patty? Does it look as if they're friends?

During reading

- Let your child read at their own pace – don't worry if it's slow. They could read silently, or read to you out loud.
- Help them to work out words they don't know by saying each sound out loud and then blending them to say the word, e.g. *b-oul-d-er, boulder.*
- If your child still struggles with a word, just tell them the word and move on.
- Give them lots of praise for good reading!

After reading

- Look at page 32 for some fun activities.

Chapter One

It was a sunny afternoon in Volcano
Valley. The dinosaurs had met
next to the lake. They were going
to play boulder ball. Steggs and Tricky
were the team captains.

"I want to be a captain," squeaked
Cosmo. He was the smallest dinosaur.

"Don't be silly," laughed the others.
"You're not big enough."

"It shouldn't matter how big I am!"
said Cosmo.

The dinosaurs stood in a line.
The captains picked teams.
Cosmo and Patty were picked last.
Nobody wanted them.
Cosmo was too small.
And Patty was too slow.

The captains chose a boulder.
Then the game began.

Cosmo and Patty tried to get the
boulder. They tried very hard.
Patty ran after it. But she was too slow.
Someone else always got there first.

Cosmo could get to the boulder. But he was too small. He couldn't move it — no matter how hard he tried. The other dinosaurs laughed at him.

"It's not fair," said Cosmo. "If I were captain, I'd choose a small boulder. One that everyone could play with."

Just then, a dreadful roar echoed
across the valley.

"Oh, no!" wailed Steggs. "It's Tyro!"

Tyro was a terrible tyrannosaur. She
was always gobbling up other dinosaurs.

"Quick!" shrieked Tricky. "We'd better
hide – or she will eat us."

The dinosaurs ran off. Patty and Cosmo were left by the lake.

Patty was very scared. She was too big to hide and too slow to run. Her large eyes filled with tears.

"Don't wait for me, Cosmo," she said sadly. "You had better go and hide."

Cosmo was scared, too. But he stuck by his friend and thought fast.

"Don't worry," he said. "We'll be all right."

Chapter Two

The ground shook and the lake shivered
as Tyro stomped into the valley.

Her mouth and claws were dripping
with blood.

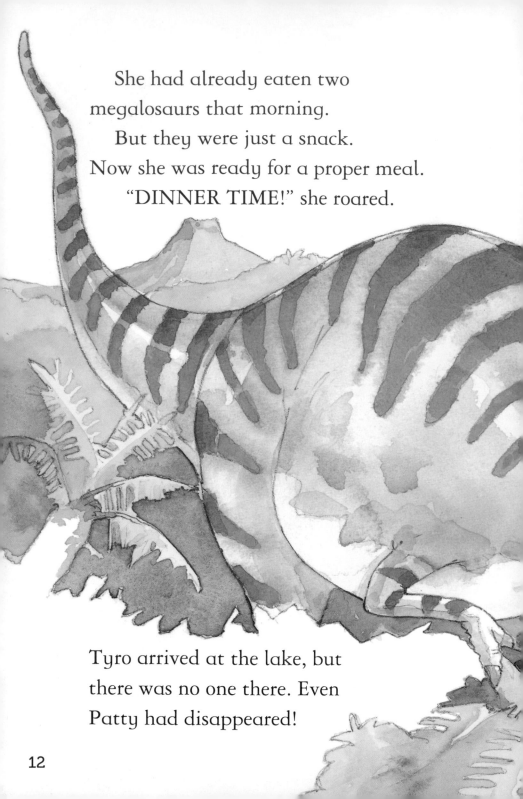

She had already eaten two
megalosaurs that morning.
　　But they were just a snack.
Now she was ready for a proper meal.
　　"DINNER TIME!" she roared.

Tyro arrived at the lake, but
there was no one there. Even
Patty had disappeared!

Tyro was not stupid. She knew the dinosaurs were hiding, and she knew how to find them.

"What shall I have to eat?" she said, as if thinking out loud. "A juicy iguanodon? Or a fat triceratops? No! What I REALLY fancy is a crunchy STEGOSAURUS!"

The dinosaurs were hiding behind a pile of rocks.

Steggs heard Tyro say that she was going to eat him. He was very, very scared.

He trembled so much that the plates on his back were rattling.

"Shush," whispered the other dinosaurs. "Tyro will hear you."

But it was too late. Tyro was already
coming towards them.

Tyro had almost reached the pile of
rocks, when she heard a squeaky voice.

"Hey, SWAMP-BREATH! If you want
to pick on someone, why not pick on me?"

Tyro looked round
and saw Cosmo.
He was dancing up
and down next to
the lake.

"Don't be silly," snorted Tyro.
"I wouldn't waste my time chasing you.
You are only a little mouthful."

And she turned back towards
the rocks.

Chapter Three

Tyro had almost found the other dinosaurs, when Cosmo called out again.

"You tyrannosaurs are all the same," he said. "If someone stands up to you, you run off with your tail between your legs."

Tyro stopped in her tracks.

"WHAT DID YOU SAY?" she snarled.

"You heard me," yelled Cosmo.
"You're a SCAREDY-SAURUS!"

"THAT'S ENOUGH!" shouted Tyro.
"I'll show you who's a scaredy-saurus."
The tyrannosaur swung around and
stormed towards the lake.

Cosmo did not look frightened. But
he was just pretending. He was really
very scared.

Tyro's huge jaws
swooped down.

It looked as if he
was going to be
snapped up! He was
going to be chewed
into a thousand
soggy pieces!

But Cosmo
didn't run away!

At the last moment, Cosmo jumped backwards into the lake.

He landed on a small island, close to the shore.

"Come on, CLUMSY-CLAWS," he yelled. "Come and get me. If you dare."

Tyro hesitated. She didn't like water. But the island was very close to the shore.

"Hey, FOSSIL-FACE. What's the matter?" shouted Cosmo. He waved his tiny fists. "Are you a scaredy-saurus after all?"

That settled it.

Tyro wasn't going to be called any more names. She charged into the water and waded towards the island.

The other dinosaurs peered out from their hiding place. They were amazed by what was happening.

"What does Cosmo think he's doing?" asked Tricky. "Has he gone mad?"

"And where is Patty?" asked Steggs.

Tyro thrashed through the water towards Cosmo.

The little dinosaur was still laughing. The more Cosmo laughed, the angrier Tyro got. She was so angry, she didn't notice that Cosmo's island was MOVING.

It was leading her further and further into the lake.

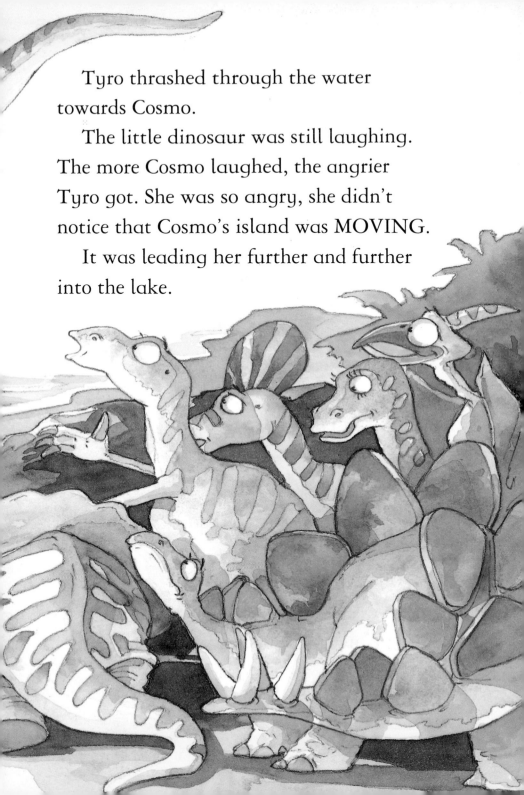

Chapter Four

All of a sudden, Tyro was up to her neck in water.

"HELP! HELP! I CAN'T SWIM!" she shrieked.

"Oh dear," said Cosmo. He wasn't scared any more. "I don't suppose you want my help. I'm only a *little mouthful*."

"PLEASE!" howled Tyro. "I'll do anything you want."

"Anything?" asked Cosmo.

"Anything," spluttered Tyro.

"Do you promise to leave our valley and never come back?"

"Yes! Yes! I promise," gurgled Tyro. She was desperate. "Just get me out of this water."

"All right, then," said Cosmo.
He stamped his foot on the island.
Patty's head popped out of the water
next to him.

Then, everyone realized what
had happened.

Cosmo wasn't standing on a real
island. He was standing on Patty's back!
That was how she had disappeared.
That was why the island had been moving.

Patty dragged Tyro back to the shore.

The other dinosaurs had come out from their hiding place. They were clapping and cheering.

Tyro felt terrible. She hated being laughed at. She struggled to her feet. Then she trudged out of the valley, without saying a word.

The dinosaurs thanked Cosmo and
Patty for saving them.

"I thought I was going to be eaten,"
said Steggs.

"I would never have dared to lead Tyro
into the lake," said Tricky.

"It was all Cosmo's idea," said Patty. "He's the one you should thank."

"Nonsense," said Cosmo. "I could never have done it without Patty. It was just good teamwork."

"Now, what happened to our game of boulder ball?" asked Cosmo.

"I think we should start again," said Steggs.

"With new captains," said Tricky.

"Someone who will look after their whole team," agreed Steggs.

"COSMO AND PATTY!" shouted all the others.

After reading activities

Quick quiz

See how fast you can answer these questions!
Look back at the story if you can't remember.

 1 Who were the team captains at the start?

 2 Why did **Cosmo** lead **Tyro** into the lake?

 3 Why did **Tyro** leave the valley in the end?

Talk about it!

- Do you think **Cosmo** will be a good team captain? Why?

- Do you think **Tyro** will ever come back to the valley?

1) Steggs and Tricky; 2) because it was away from the other dinosaurs, and Cosmo knew he could trick Tyro; 3) she didn't like being laughed at